Rocket Writes

To Jonanna, who is optimistic and always
supportive and loves to laugh at a good story

Copyright © 2012 by Tad Hills
All rights reserved. Published in
the United States by Schwartz & Wade Books, an
imprint of Random House Children's Books,
a division of Random House, Inc., New York.
Schwartz & Wade Books and the colophon are
trademarks of Random House, Inc.
Visit us on the Web! randomhouse.com/kids
Educators and librarians, for a variety of teaching
tools, visit us at randomhouse.com/teachers
Library of Congress Cataloging-in-Publication Data
Hills, Tad.
Rocket writes a story /
Tad Hills. — 1st ed.   p. cm.
Sequel to: How Rocket learned to read.
Summary: "Rocket writes a story about a new
friend, the owl"—Provided by publisher.

ISBN 978-0-375-87086-6 (trade)
ISBN 978-0-375-97086-3 (glb)
[1. Authorship—Fiction. 2. Books and reading—Fiction.
3. Dogs—Fiction. 4. Owls—Fiction. 5. Birds—Fiction.]
I. Title.
PZ7.H563737Roc 2012
[E]—dc23
2011041233
The text of this book is set in Tyrnavia.
The illustrations were rendered in oil paint
and colored pencil.
MANUFACTURED IN CHINA
10 9 8 7 6 5 4 3 2 1
First Edition

a Story by Tad Hills

schwartz & wade books · new york

Rocket loved books. He loved to read them to himself or to sit quietly by his teacher, the little yellow bird, as she read them aloud.

Rocket even liked the way books smelled. When he opened a new book, it smelled like a place he'd never been to, like a friend he'd never met.

The little yellow bird agreed. "Books are inspiring! They make me sing."

Rocket loved words, too. After snack time his teacher would say, "Rocket, why don't you use that nose of yours to sniff out some new words?"

And off he'd go. He'd fetch some nice ones like *buttercup*,

and *bug*,

and *feather*,

and *nest*.

"I'm looking for words,"
Rocket would announce to
anyone who'd listen.

Rocket always brought his words back to the classroom and wrote them down. The little yellow bird would help him spell the tricky ones, and then they'd hang them on their word tree.

Sometimes the bird added her own words to the collection. "This one is small, but I promise it'll come in handy," she'd say.

"Magnificent!" chirped the little yellow bird once their tree was covered. "Now what shall we do with all these splendid words?"
Rocket thought all afternoon. Then he had an idea.

Rocket left school that day with a very waggy tail. "I'm going to write a story!" he declared to Fred and Emma.

"My story will be an adventure about the great wide world," he told a butterfly.

"I will use many words,"
he explained to Mr. Barker.

"Hello up there!" he called as he passed the tree where he had found the word *nest*. "I'm going to write a story!"

The next day, Rocket returned
to his classroom. It was time to begin. He
looked down at the blank page and the blank
page looked up at him. But no story would come.

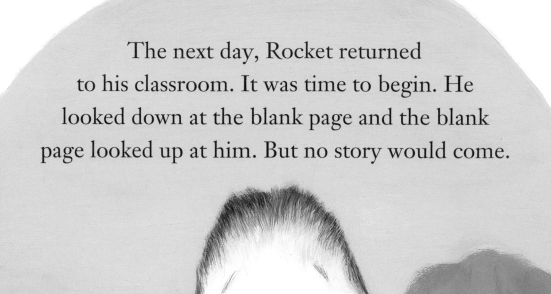

At snack time, Rocket gave up. "I don't know what to write," he told his teacher.

"Don't worry," the little yellow bird replied. "One of the hardest parts of writing is coming up with a good story. But it's one of the most fun, too. Perhaps you want to write about something you've seen."

"A bug?" asked Rocket.

"Yes!" sang his teacher. "Stories need good characters. Or what about something that happened to you? Or something you really enjoy?"

"My favorite stick?" suggested Rocket.

"Of course!" said the bird. "Or you could write about something that inspires you!"

"*Inspires* me?" asked Rocket.

"Yes, something that excites you," the little yellow bird sang.

Rocket took a walk and looked for inspiration. He thought about friends he knew and places he'd been. He stuck his nose high in the air and sniffed the gentle breeze. And there it was— a delightful smell of pine needles and feathers. Inspiration!

For the rest of the morning he thought about feathers and pine needles. Pine needles and feathers.

That afternoon he started to write.

In the evening Rocket followed the beautiful smell until he found himself at the tree with the nest.

"Hello again," he called into the branches. "Is anyone home?"

He heard rustling from above, but no one answered.

"I'm sorry to disturb you, but . . . I must tell you that you smell nice. Very inspiring. May I ask who you are?"

Still nothing. "Perhaps I'll come back at a more convenient time," he said, and trotted off.

That night, as Rocket watched the stars, he thought about feathers and a nest in a pine tree. He thought about his story and his collection of words.

On his way to school the next day, Rocket was surprised by what he saw.

"A brand-new word!" he said. "And it's already written down. It says . . ." He tried to sound the word out.

"*Owl*," came a quiet voice from the branches. "It says *owl*. That's me."

"Thank you, Owl," Rocket called. "I'm always looking for words, and this one's a beauty!"

Rocket ran all the way to his classroom.

"*O-W-L, owl*. Now, there's a word you don't hear every day," chirped the little yellow bird. "Only three letters, but what a word!"

"It was a present," explained Rocket, and he added the new word to his story.

"I'm writing a story about you," Rocket announced proudly to the owl the next morning.

The owl poked her head out of her nest, and for the first time Rocket saw her friendly face. Her big round eyes blinked below feathery tufts. "About me?" she asked softly.

"Would you like to come down and hear it?" asked Rocket.

"Thank you, but I think I'll listen from my nest," the owl answered.

So Rocket cleared his throat and began to read. "Once there was an owl. She smelled like feathers and pine needles. She lived in a tree."

The owl's eyes widened. "Is there more?"

"There will be," said Rocket.

Each day Rocket worked
on his story. He wrote words
down and crossed words out.
When things were going well,
he wagged his tail.

When he didn't know
what to write,
he growled.

Sometimes he drew pictures for his story

or took a walk in the meadow to look for inspiration.

The little yellow bird encouraged him.
"Remember, stories take time," she'd say.

She wanted to know more about the owl and asked Rocket questions. "Why do you think the owl wouldn't come down? What color is her beak? What does she do every day?"

Rocket wanted to know more about the owl, too. He visited her tree often and read her his story, which changed every day.

The owl was captivated.

And when
Rocket stopped,
she would always
ask, "Then what
happened?"

At last came the day when Rocket knew he was finished.

"What a fine story!" chirped the little yellow bird after she'd read it.

My First Story
by Rocket

Rocket ran to the owl's pine tree.

"It's done!" he called. "Come listen!"

And so down and down came the owl, till she was right beside Rocket.

Then Rocket began to read. He read about an owl with friendly eyes and a beak the color of a buttercup. She lived in a nest high in a tree on the edge of a meadow and smelled like pine needles and feathers. She liked to nap in the daytime and listen to stories.

"Branch by branch, the owl came down from her nest,"
Rocket read. "She was shy, but she was brave, too."

Suddenly, Rocket stopped. He wrote something on his
paper, then began to read again. "One day the owl came
all the way to the ground and became my friend."

The owl blinked. "Can there be one last sentence?" she asked. "Can you say, 'And the owl liked the story very much'?"

"What a perfect ending!" said Rocket.

And it was.